The Hungry S

Story by Annette Smith

Illustrations by Jenny Mountstephen

Rigby
A Harcourt Achieve Imprint

www.Rigby.com
1-800-531-5015

Little Squirrel is up

in a big tree.

He is hungry.

3

Little Squirrel can see a basket on the big tree.

Here comes Little Squirrel.

Look at Little Squirrel.

He is in the basket.

He is looking for nuts.

Little Squirrel sees a nut

in the basket.

Look at the basket!

A girl is looking

at Little Squirrel.

Little Squirrel is looking

at the girl.

He can see the nuts.

The nuts are for

the hungry squirrel.